"Would you come with us, please?"

Two men brandishing assault rifles pointed them directly at Kyle and Rachel.

"She's not going anywhere with you," Kyle said. "You'll have to go through me first." He moved to position Rachel behind him, and they fired a round at his feet.

"We don't mind doing that," the man snickered, "but Rachel could save your life if she merely came with us."

Kyle glanced sideways, trying to take in Rachel's demeanor. Her jaw was set tight and her nostrils flared.

Her body was priming for a fight.

"Rachel, if you don't get into the van right now, Mr. Reid gets a bullet."

Kyle went for his gun but couldn't pull it in time. At first, he didn't hear the gunshot, but he felt the hot projectile slice through his flesh. Warm, thick fluids dripped down his side and he pressed his hand to the wound to stop the bleeding.

When he had a moment to gain focus back on the street, he saw Rachel stepping inside the van.

"Rachel, no!"

Jordyn Redwood is a pediatric ER nurse by day, suspense novelist by night. She pursued her dream of becoming an author by first penning her medical thrillers *Proof*, *Poison* and *Peril*. Jordyn hosts *Redwood's Medical Edge*, a blog helping authors write medically accurate fiction. Living near the Rocky Mountains with her husband, two beautiful daughters and one crazy dog provides inspiration for her books. She loves to get emails from her readers at jredwood1@gmail.com.

Books by Jordyn Redwood

Love Inspired Suspense

Fractured Memory
Taken Hostage
Fugitive Spy
Christmas Baby Rescue
Eliminating the Witness

Visit the Author Profile page at LoveInspired.com.

ELIMINATING THE WITNESS

JORDYN REDWOOD

LOVE INSPIRED SUSPENSE

INSPIRATIONAL ROMANCE

LOVE INSPIRED® SUSPENSE
INSPIRATIONAL ROMANCE

ISBN-13: 978-1-335-58850-0

Eliminating the Witness

Copyright © 2023 by Jordyn Redwood

Recycling programs
for this product may
not exist in your area.

For questions and comments about the quality of this book, please contact us at CustomerService@Harlequin.com.

Love Inspired
22 Adelaide St. West, 41st Floor
Toronto, Ontario M5H 4E3, Canada
www.LoveInspired.com

Printed in U.S.A.

And ye shall know the truth,
and the truth shall make you free.
—*John* 8:32

For Marcella Shadle. Thank you for speaking Truth
into my life and for praying for me...always.

ONE

"Have you seen this woman?"

Rachel Bright stopped as the man shoved the piece of paper into her face. She stepped back and plucked it from his fingertips, viewing the photo on the flyer.

It was her.

At least, the person she once was. The scared shell of a woman who had been married to one of the most prolific, most feared—and most admired—serial killers of all time.

She covered her throat with her free hand to hide her racing heartbeat. Now, three years later, she didn't resemble the woman in the photo anymore, and the man searching didn't realize he was staring into the eyes of his quarry. Her hair was now dyed blond and worn longer, instead of the short, dark brown pixie cut it used to be. Dropping fifty pounds of weight had thinned her features. The only thing similar to the woman in the photo was the haunted look, which was now shielded by her mirrored sunglasses.

"Why are you trying to find her?" Rachel asked, handing the flyer back.

"You've seen her, then?" the man asked, placing the piece of paper back on his pile.

"No, but I work EMS in the area and would be interested in knowing if this woman is in danger." Rachel shifted her backpack higher on her shoulder and gripped the strap tighter to shield her shaking body from the stranger. Her years working in emergency medicine had made her an expert at hiding her feelings during a crisis in order to stay focused on the situation at hand.

And this was a looming catastrophe of monumental proportions. Some would say an existential threat.

"She's missing. Has been for three years," the man said.

"Who reported her missing?"

That question was like a hand smothering the man's mouth, silencing his words. No matter. Unbeknownst to him, Rachel knew what the truth was. No one had reported her missing. She'd been expertly hidden in the Witness Protection Program after her testimony had guaranteed her ex-husband served multiple life sentences for his crimes. The only people who ever looked for her were journalists scavenging for her side of the story or members of her ex-husband's cult following, who blamed her for putting a man they thought innocent in jail.

Or those who knew of his crimes and admired him for it. People were complicated.

The man chose not to respond to her question. Instead he asked again, "Have you seen her?"

"I haven't, but I'll let you know if I do." Rachel checked his shoulder as she brushed past him. Perhaps because of the pent-up anger over how her ex-husband, aka the Black Death, had forever altered the lives of so many women, including hers.

At least she was still alive.

"Let me give you my number," the man called after her.

Rachel did not turn around. At nearly every lamppost was her photo staring back at her. Still more people were handing out the photo to passersby. Rachel lifted the hood of her black windbreaker, further shielding her face. The wisdom of reporting to work when so many were seeking her made her steps cautious. How much longer would her changed appearance mystify those searching—no, hunting her down?

She reached for her cell phone, pulling up the contact number for Kyle Reid, the WIT-SEC inspector who had placed her in protective custody. It had been three years since they'd been in contact. He'd been the one anchor that had held her together during the trial. One of the few men, maybe the only man, she would call trustworthy. He'd held together her broken pieces while the world called for charges to be brought against her—assuming without evidence that she was complicit in her ex-husband's crimes. Calling Kyle would set her on a course of action she didn't feel ready for. A new identity. A new life and starting over again. She'd grown to love Springdale, Utah. It was the place where she found herself again—the true core of who she was—stripped down from all the accouterments of the two-physician-salary lifestyle she'd led before. Back then, she'd felt like she'd been living the American dream, until it all crumbled around her when, at their remote cabin, she'd found her then husband and the woman he'd imprisoned there for months. That was only the tip of the iceberg.

Shutting out the memories, she quickened her pace. There was one street that emptied into Zion National Park. The EMS substation was close to the base. Though the morning was cool, temperatures this summer were hitting record highs.

She put the phone back in her pocket. Her fingers tingled at her decision. Why were people looking for her now? As the result of being in witness protection, she'd intentionally stayed away from social media platforms. She kept one computer, for doing online research, but she tried to keep her digital footprint nonexistent, which meant not logging onto many of the popular sites for news. Breaking news rarely reached her until she got her newspaper the next day. Old-school but sufficient for her needs. One national publication was all she allowed herself.

Before she knew it, her feet had taken her to the base. Even though she'd refrained from developing close friendships with people, there was a camaraderie with her team that she enjoyed.

"Mornin', Rachel."

"Hey, Moose." The EMT had been so nick-named for his bulky size. He readily owned it. Rachel didn't know what his legal name was, but he'd carried the nickname since his NFL linebacker years. His strength was useful when they had to carry people down off trails.

"How did nights fare?" Rachel asked as she approached her locker, opening the metal door and placing her backpack inside.

"Fairly qu—"

"Moose! You know we never utter that word. How many times do I have to tell you?"

He waved her complaint away. "If it's gonna be a bad day, nothin' I say is gonna keep it from coming. By the way, someone came here looking for you. Left you this." Moose reached out and handed her an envelope.

She opened it and read the words, printed in prim block letters.

I NEED TO TALK TO YOU TODAY. I'LL BE BACK AT THE END OF YOUR SHIFT. HEATHER.

Rachel shoved the note back into the envelope. Why had Heather, the only victim of Seth's found alive, come here? Maybe the Black Crew had followed her, which could explain why they were canvassing the area.

Her reconstructed life was going to end. She was going to have to start over. Sadness enveloped her. A tightness at the base of her throat made it difficult to breathe. This was going to be her last day with the team of people she'd grown to love. People she thought of as family.

Moose's question startled her. "Did you see all those people in town? Looking for that woman?"

Rachel swallowed hard. "I did. Know anything about it? They say she's missing."

"Well, I don't know if *missing* would be the right word. Hiding is more like it."

"What do you mean?"

"Her ex murdered a lot of women. He's ranked as one of the top ten serial killers. Estimated to have killed nearly fifty women. She went into witness protection after she testified against him."

"You...followed the case?"

"Who didn't follow the case is a better question."

The station tones sounded, and a voice rang out in the room. "Gunshot wound. Base of Emerald Pools."

"Did I hear that right?" Moose said. "Gunshot wound?"

"Like I said...never use the *Q* word."

"Easier to grab our stuff and run there," Moose said as he straightened up from tying his hiking boots. "It's right across the way."

Rachel grabbed a trauma pack and followed him out the door. Moose yelled back for the other two techs to bring the rig.

On a sunny summer day, there were plenty of people on the trails trying to beat the heat. As soon as Rachel and Moose crossed the main road to get to the trailhead, a stream of people was coming at them. In the distance, they could hear the distinct sound of gunfire.

Moose grabbed Rachel's shoulder. "It's an active shooter. We need to wait for the police."

It was a standard in EMS—to wait to provide help until law enforcement deemed the scene safe. An injured or dead rescuer wasn't a help to anyone. Rachel couldn't abide by it at that moment. Knew she'd be in trouble once the chief heard about it, but she couldn't stand by and wait. No sense in worrying about being fired when she wouldn't be working there anymore.

"You wait here for them," Rachel instructed. "I'm going to go up and see if there are any victims."

"Rachel..."

More gunshots. "I'm not asking you to go with me."

"Yeah, but you know I'm also not going to let you leave me behind. Chief's gonna be mad if we die. He'll kill us again."

Moose behind her, Rachel jogged up the trail, stepping to the side as people raced down. Once people saw their medical attire, they pointed back on the trail, evidently signaling where the victim lay.

The trail narrowed. It was going to be difficult to do any work to save a life sandwiched between rock walls and thorny underbrush. That's when they saw her, alone, lain out like a child doing a snow angel. A plume of red on her chest. Rachel closed the distance quickly, her first instinct to place her hand against the woman's wound, a few inches under her left collarbone, to stem the bleeding.

"Ma'am, can you hear me?" Rachel called to her, reaching for her face and turning her toward her. Was she still breathing?

"Rachel…"

It was Heather…the last known of Seth's victims found alive at their cabin after weeks of imprisonment and torture. The other woman responsible for putting her husband behind bars.

* * *

Kyle Reid had just stepped out of his parked car when he heard the gunshots ring out. His stomach clenched. Hopefully, Rachel wasn't involved. He had to find her before something happened, and he was already nervous about the number of people he'd encountered who were looking for her. Hurrying from the parking lot, he ran through the stream of people charging against him to get away from the danger.

His standard-issue suit and tie with dress shoes did little for his agility on the sandy trail. Quickly, he shed his jacket and threw it off to the side, which exposed his firearm. Several people glanced his way, and it only made them run faster. He stepped in front of one woman and grabbed her by the shoulders.

"I'm a US marshal. Where is the shooter?"

The woman shivered underneath his palms. "I don't know, exactly. Not too far up the trail. There's a woman—she's injured…"

He dropped his hands, and she scurried away. Another few pops from the weapon forced his feet to move. The people running away had thinned out, making it easier for him to forge up the path.

As he took a hairpin turn, he saw a para-